CW00864059

Lest We Forget

Lest We Forget

An Anthology of Remembrance

Brian L Porter

Published 2014 by Creativia

Book design by Creativia (www.creativia.org)

Cover art by http://www.thecovercollection.com/

Foreword

Brian L. Porter is perhaps better known as the author of the award-winning novel 'A Study in Red – The Secret Journal of Jack the Ripper, and other thrillers of a similar ilk. Also a screenwriter and co-producer for ThunderBall Films of Los Angeles, what is little known, however, is that the author is also a successful and accomplished poet, having won the Preditors & Editors 'Best Poet of 2008 Award' under one of his pseudonyms, Juan Pablo Jalisco.

Here, under his own name is a superb collection of poetry of war and remembrance, pieced together over the author's many years of working with and writing about the various ex-servicemen's associations, with which he has been connected over a long period of time, following his service in the Royal Air Force.

Also by Brian L Porter

- A Study in Red – The Secret Journal of Jack the Ripper
  Winner, The Preditors & Editors Best Thriller Novel of 2008 Award

- Legacy of the Ripper

- Requiem for the Ripper

- Behind Closed Doors

- Kiss of Life

- The Nemesis Cell

- Avenue of the Dead

- Purple Death

- Pestilence

- Glastonbury

- The Voice of Anton Bouchard

- Of Aztecs and Conquistadors (As Juan Pablo Jalisco)

- A Binary Convergence (With Graeme S Houston)

Introduction

I have been privileged, in recent years, to have met and talked with many surviving soldiers and airmen who took part in some of the most momentous periods of our recent history. As the memories of the 20th century's world wars recede in the public mind, I have attempted to record, in verse, some of the experiences of those brave men who made our present, comfortable world possible. Each of the poems you are about to read is based on the personal experience of an individual soldier or airman, or relates to a documented event in history. I have not attempted to glorify war. This is a work of remembrance, a small way of trying to convey to the reader the debt we owe to the men and women who, in many cases, paid the ultimate sacrifice in defence of their homeland.

I owe a debt of gratitude to the many people who have provided me with the inspiration for much of this work, but, in particular, I wish to record my thanks to Jacqui Whitehead, Jim Bulmer, the gentlemen of the Doncaster branch of the Air Gunners Association, (especially the late Steve Green and Jimmy Goldie D.F.C., D.F.M.), for their wonderful reminiscences, and the members of the Doncaster Central branch of the Royal British Legion, without whose help this collection would not have been possible, and finally, a special thank you to my Mother, Enid Porter, my greatest supporter, to whom this work is dedicated!

Kiss of Death

Welcome to the carnival, the carnival of carnage!
Welcome to the Reaper's realm, where death's stormtroopers forage.
Welcome to destruction, to blood, and guts, and tears.
Welcome to the final resting place of all your fears.

To mighty confrontation, to awesome total war,
Where bodies hang on branches like the blood on Satan's claw.
Where blood flows like a tide of tears, where oblivion is bliss,
Welcome to the carnival, come, feel the bullet's kiss!

From the Trenches

Death, you walk among us every day, I fear you not.
You bring with you a sweet relief to those too tired too escape
you.
No more mud, no more stench, no more whistles.
"Up and at 'em boys", over the top, kill the Hun, what fun!

Shattered bodies, bullets flying, "Look out boys, it's gas".
Torment, beyond our realms of belief,
For this we left our Mothers' breast,
For England, God, and King.

Earth stained red with rotting corpses,
We couldn't stop and bring them back.
I'm sorry Mother, I really am,
We wanted to, we really did.

"Over by Christmas", someone said,
Not this year boys, and maybe never.
We'll go on dancing the dance of death,
Why not, it's a lovely war!

Casualties of War

Marching proudly off to war, wearing uniforms with pride,
Within a few weeks most were gone, innocence had died.
Cannon fodder for the guns, casualties of battle,
Victims of the politics that made the sabres rattle!

The generals told them "Worry not, the war will not last long",
They left their homes and families, and sang the soldiers song.
But the long-laid plans of generals were just a bitter seed,
That reaped a bitter harvest, as they watched their manhood
bleed!

They were men like any other, they were fathers, brothers, sons,
Sacrificed by those who never heard the fire of guns!
Loyal and patriotic, for their generals they died well,
As they coughed their life-blood out within that man-created
Hell!

Rain and mud, and heat and dust, the seasons passed on by,
As months rolled into years beneath that smoke enveloped sky!
In that place they called the battlefield, they lived, and fought,
and died,
In homes throughout the nation, many mothers wept and cried.

For the soldiers of the Kaiser, who had fought the generals' war,
They had faced the British "Tommy", they had heard the Lions
roar.
At last the guns fell silent, and the Sun rose once again,
They shuffled home, but now they seemed, an army of old men.

No victory parades, and no sabres left to rattle,
Just the memories of the men they'd known, lost in futile battle!

Of horrors now they must forget, never to repeat,
Let not the generals plan again, the sound of marching feet!

Young Georgie, Soldier of the King

He was sixteen years old, but now Georgie is dead,
He told lies 'bout his age, he was shot through the head.
He wore the Kings uniform, bursting with pride,
'Til, his blood stained the ground on the day that he died.

Thick acrid smoke clung low to the ground,
As the company waited for the whistle to sound.
The sounds of the battle around them were loud,
As they waited to walk through that cannon-made shroud.

Young Georgie was nervous, excited as well,
They all knew that soon they'd be pitched into Hell.
Where kill or be killed was the only way out,
Still they waited for the whistle, the officer's shout.

Some said a prayer, and some shook with fear,
The sergeant just stood there, scratching his ear.
Then the sound of the whistle, and "over the top",
Georgie knew this was it, he'd gone too far to stop.

So brave and so gallant, they charged at the Hun,
They wouldn't relent 'til the battle was won.
The earth all around them was stained with the blood,
Of the dead and the dying, the brave, and the good.

Young Georgie was hit only yards from the trench,
He fell to the ground, in the blood and the stench.
As his life ebbed away in that terrible place,
His last thoughts were of home, of his dear Mother's face.

He was hailed as a hero, by the people at home,
But his Mother just cried for the fruit of her womb.
Young Georgie lies buried in a soldiers grave,
For King and for country his future he gave.

He left home as a boy, but he died as a man,
He gave all that he had, all that anyone can.
To this day in his home town, the story is told,
Of a brave English soldier, just sixteen years old!

Holocaust

Condemned by doctrine fuelled by hate,
How many passed through Auschwitz'gate?
Treblinka, Belsen, Sachsenhausen,
Trains brought victims by the thousand.

Innocent of any crime,
But this was Europe's' darkest time.
Black legions of the evil one,
Obliterated freedoms' sun.

Deprived of every human need,
Mutilated, left to bleed!
Experiments upon the living,
By so-called doctors, unforgiving.

Beaten, tortured, past belief,
The rich, the poor, conjoined in grief.
Tried to survive another day,
To God in Heaven above they'd pray!

Girl and boy, woman, man,
Slaves of this Satanic clan.
Mothers, fathers, daughters, sons,
Behind barbed wire, faced with guns.

Waiting, naked, in the cold,
The living dead, young and old.
"Selections", sentences of death,
Gas, Zyclon "B", last choking breath.

Those belching crematoria
Cast human dust into the air.
Like furnaces of earthly hell,
Would anyone be left to tell?

To tell the tale of Hell on Earth,
Where "Final Solution" was given birth.
Where Hitler's' inhumanity,
Bred national insanity!

So when the day of freedom came,
Was then revealed a nation's shame.
Survivors of the Holocaust,
Told of families, millions lost!

A generation all but gone,
A few survived to carry on.
To live and tell of what took place,
When mankind lost its human face.

Emaciated, living ghosts,
Sought new homes, appealed for hosts.
Scoured the world for sanctuary,
Adjusting now, to being free.

Some of those victims still survive,
A miracle that they're alive!
Remembering, it must be said,
Mothers, Fathers, long since dead!

Children once, now old and grey,
They never had a chance to play.
Surrounded by the wire and towers,
No toys, no games, no Springtime flowers.

The tears are real as heavy hearted,
Prayers are said for those long departed.
Their testament is in survival,
Of their peoples' continued revival.

The lessons of the past are there,
A warning hanging in the air.
Mankind, don't ever justify,
That human dust, up in the sky.........!

(In remembrance of the millions)

Blitz

The sirens wailed, they were back again,
Bringing mayhem, deadly rain!
People running helter-skelter,
Tried to reach the nearest shelter.

Time and time again they came, the terror in the night,
With bombs that dropped and turned the dark sky burning
bright!
As London burned the sky took on an orange haze,
Buildings left as rubble became a twisted maze.

Last resting place for many, trapped by walls of fire,
Buried 'neath the wreckage of that ghastly funeral pyre!
Rescue workers with bare hands tried frantically to free
The injured and the dying, those who hadn't time to flee.

As fire crews worked tirelessly to stem that burning tide,
Walls fell down with fearful crash, trapping those still left inside.
With streets in total chaos, using water from the river,
To beat the flames, no matter what the enemy could deliver!

In the aftermath of chaos, through that fog of acrid smoke,
People found the bulldog spirit, found time for ironic joke.
"They've gorn and 'it the Rose and Crown" said Bill, in total horror,
"Use "The Anchor" then said Daisy, "They're re-opening it tomorrer!

They cleaned the streets, shored up the walls, and did the best they could,
In teams they shifted twisted metal, concrete, blackened wood!
Prayers were said for those no longer here amongst the living,
Babies cried, mothers wept, their tears were unforgiving.

And as nighttime came around once more, and searchlights raked the skies,
People waited for the bombers, watched with tired, weary, eyes.
Waiting for the sounds of sirens wailing once again,
Asking, when will all this end, and if it does, then when?

But never once did London's people give a thought of defeat,
We'd fight them any way we could, 'til old Hitler we'd unseat.
We'd hide beneath the city in the dear old Underground,
Then come out when it's over, when the good old "All Clear" sounds.

Bomber

Quietly waiting in misty shroud,
A bomber standing, silent, proud.
Soon, on eagles wings to fly,
Above the clouds, in darkened sky.

Bombs loaded, fuel tanks full, and then,
Your crew arrives, those gallant men ,
With parachutes, and flying suits,
Oxygen masks, and fleece lined boots.

With moon obscured by banks of cloud,
Nature grants protective shroud.
Airscrews cut through the air like knives,
As mighty merlins roar with life.

A signal flare, the time is nigh,
To leave the earth once more, to fly,
And as you slip your earthly bounds,
You fly o'er fields, and darkened towns.

Above the cloud, across the sea,
Target for tonight? Germany!
As fighters try to halt your flight,
Bright tracer trails light up the night!

Determinedly your crew fights back,
Successfully repel attack.
Now flak bursts terrorise your frame,
The next round in your deadly game.

You turn for home with bombs away,
Again the fighters have their say.
A hit takes out port outer engine,
You're limping now, crew feel the tension.

Through the darkness, through the night,
Losing speed, losing height.
Will you make it? Crewmen pray,
God help us to survive this day.

Though now the clouds you fly below,
Coughing, creaking, ever slow,
You're over England's fields once more,
Gaping hole in your cockpit floor!

Though sorely wounded, twisted, battered,
You made it back, that's all that mattered.
They'll patch you up and send you back,
You're needed for the next attack!

But, until then you'll stand at ease,
As ground crews serve your every need.
Bomber, chariot of war,
Sleep, 'til your engines roar once more!

A salute to the men, the women and the aircraft of Royal Air
Force Bomber Command.

Polska

See the old man as he walks down the street,
Walking unsteadily, shuffling his feet.
The children still laugh at his accent you know,
They wouldn't have laughed sixty years ago.

He came here from Poland, he came here to fight,
He flew in a bomber, night after night.
In Hampdens and Wellingtons, Lancaster's too,
Through year after year of wartime he flew.

He never sought medals, he never sought fame,
Just wanted his home to see freedom again.
To talk to his father, his sister, his brother,
To feel safe again in the arms of his mother.

He knew hope, he knew fear, and with each passing mission,
Never once did the young man regret his decision,
To flee from his country, escape tyranny,
And fight for a world that was peaceful and free.

Cold nights over Germany, Essen, the Ruhr,
The relief of surviving another tour.
He lived on his nerves till the end of the war,
Till the bombers and fighters were needed no more.

Now he sits and remembers, and sometimes with pride,
Recalls friends and comrades, so many who died.
Of those who survived, they like him now are old,
And seldom today is their story told.

How they came here and flew, and they fought, and they died,
How they came and they danced, laughed, and sang, and they cried.
As they see today's' conflicts, and bitter exchanges,
They must wonder if anything really changes.

Now the young man has aged, and he lives all alone,
Wife died a while ago, children have grown.
See the old man as he walks down the street,
Walking unsteadily, shuffling his feet...........

Inspired by Stanislau (Stanley) Kocuba, Air Gunner, and dedicated to the men and women of the Polish forces, both at home and abroad, who fought bravely and with much sacrifice during the conflict from 1939 -1945.

Images of War

Blackout curtains, "Put out that light",
Young men marching off to fight.
Mothers waving at the door,
These were the images of war.

Home Guard parade outside the station,
Ready to repel invasion.
Broom handles and pitchforks posed as guns,
No worries, they'd repel the Huns.

Lines of young evacuees,
Grubby faces, dirty knees.
The Blitz, a bloody, smoking pyre,
As London set the night on fire.

Bismarck and Tirpitz inspired dread,
The Hood went down, so many dead!
Wolf-packs, U-Boats by the score,
These were the images of war.

Churchill's speeches, rallying cries,
The Battle of Britain fought in the skies.
So much owed to the gallant few,
They did it all for me, and you.

Atlantic convoys, cold as ice,
The merchantmen with death would dice,
Torpedoed to the ocean floor,
These were the images of war.

In Europe, Africa, and Asia,
Soldiers daily lived with danger.
Naval battles made the news,
And rationing caused awful queues.

The Burma railway, River Kwai,
Why did so many have to die?
Auschwitz, sordid infamy,
A testament to inhumanity.

Black rimmed telegrams, mothers tears,
A nation united by its fears.
Vera Lynn, doodle bugs, and more,
These were the images of war!

"Apres Moi, le Deluge"

(A tribute to 617 Squadron, Royal Air Force)

Briefing over, time to go,
A last cigarette, then 'twas on with the show.
Almost twenty to ten, the first wave took flight,
617 embarked on their dambusting night!

Determined, yet anxious, they all knew the score,
That this was a vital mission of war.
One hundred and thirty three men, brave and true,
On that dark night in May into history flew!

Through the darkness of night, they flew ever onward,
To the dams of the Ruhr, the target to be conquered.
Their minds set, and focused, on what they must do,
As the flak burst around them, still onward they flew.

On the way to the dams, five were shot from the sky,
On a night when the squadron saw fifty three die!
Ordinary young men, now remembered by name,
In the annals of history's own hall of fame.

With no thought of the cost to themselves they pressed on,
They attacked, they succeeded, the job was well done!
The bouncing bombs bounced, the dams they were breached,
They set course for a home that some still never reached.

Nineteen Lancaster bombers had left Scampton that night,
Eight failed to return from their most famous flight.
The lucky ones came back, and with the light of the dawn,
The legend of Gibson's Dambusters was born.

They will ne'er be forgot, we remember them well,
Byers, Maudslay, and Young, all the others who fell.
Regardless of rank, pilots, engineers, gunners,
Those who never came back, those who saw no more summers!

For those who were there, and for those now long gone,
Today's' squadron ensures that their memory lives on.
"Apres moi le deluge", let the legend survive,
Of the Dambusters, still here, a squadron alive!

"I am writing on behalf of all members of 617 squadron to thank you for your written tribute to "The Dambusters". It is a wonderful piece which for me captures the spirit and the courage of the young men who played a part on that fateful raid".

Flight Lieutenant Richard Saunders, 617 Squadron RAF, speaking of "Apres Moi le Deluge".

RAF Finningley, R.I.P.

Once a thriving community, now all is at peace,
This is RAF Finningley, now sadly deceased!
With runways deserted, no sound in the air,
Weeds making a home in the Signal square!
Hangars no longer put to their intended use,
Used by business for storage, a shocking abuse!
The Control Tower's boarded up, SATCO has gone,
Though the lights on the runway can still be switched on!

The guardroom's an office, they call it reception,
Doesn't quite have the ring of its designer's conception!
Poor SHQ has been stripped and laid bare,
And there's even a smell of damp in the air!
Birdsong can be heard at the Officer's Mess,
They sit on the tennis courts, perched on the nets.
In the mess footsteps echo, a single voice booms,
No carpets remain on the floors of the rooms.

The old Rose and Acorn looks sadly forlorn,
No more jollification, no more pints to be drawn.
All the people are gone who made Finningley breathe,
Retired, or posted, or on "permanent leave".
In the churchyard nearby, there's a beautiful spot,
Well tended and cared for, the RAF plot.
Where lie Finningley's fallen, at rest, and in sight
Of the place where perhaps they took their last flight!

In the village the "Harvey" is still there today,
Much quieter now since the RAF went away.
On the walls of the lounge bar the aircraft still fly,
Remember the nights when we'd drink the place dry?
For the true connoisseur of fine pie and peas,
The old "Blue Bell" of course had its own devotees.
Washed down with a Guinness, or maybe with two,
The MO swore 'twas a cure for the 'flu!

But now we're all gone, and just memories remain,
Of a friend or a colleague, or a well-loved old 'plane.
But the people who served there, we think of you yet,
Royal Air Force Finningley............we'll never forget!

Though not one of the mainstream Bomber Command bases during World War II, many of the thousand bomber raids of that conflict included aircraft flying from Finningley, many of whom failed to return. Opened as an RAF station in 1915, in its latter years Finningley became Number 6 Flying Training School and also the RAF School of navigation, until its eventual closer as an RAF base in 1996. Used for some years to house various industrial units, the airfield is now enjoying a renaissance as the current day Robin Hood International Airport, where the sound of aircraft once again fills the skies above Finningley.

The Enemy

You were my enemy, but I knew you not.
You were just a part of the plane that I shot.
Were you dark, were you fair, were you short, were you tall?
In truth, I never knew you at all.
The order to scramble came, and I went
And flew aerial ballet with you over Kent.
We twisted, and turned, we looped and we dived,
Until, by pure luck I somehow contrived

To get you in my sights, one burst, it was over,
You went down in flames in a field outside Dover!
My only thoughts then were those of elation,
Never stopping to think you were someone's relation.
The sight of your Messerschmitt spiraling down,
Brought cheers from people all over the town.
Like me they were happy, they just didn't see,
That if it hadn't been you, it would have been me.

Then after the battle my thoughts turned to you,
How, just like me, for your country you flew.
How you and your comrades had laughed in the mess,
Written letters to home, bought your sweetheart a dress.
How in many ways, enemy, you were like me,
How you wanted to fly, 'cause you wanted to be,
An airman, a pilot, a knight of the air,
Never thinking you'd meet with your death up there.

Now your death will be greeted with tears from your mother,
And with heartbreaking grief from your wife or your lover.
Your comrades in arms will drink you a toast,
Maybe spare you a thought when they next cross our coast.
And I'll think of you sometimes, my foe with no name,
How we danced in the air, how we played the same game.
I won't cheer any more when I shoot down your friends,
But I'll carry on doing it 'til the day the war ends!

Written to commemorate the 60th anniversary of the Battle of
Britain, and dedicated to the brave men and women of all nations who participated in the aerial conflict of 1940.

Ghost Squadron

I dreamed I saw in sleep last night,
Aircraft pass in silent flight.
On ghostly wings, in close formation,
Dead legions of a once proud nation!

Led by spectral wing commanders,
Flew Spitfires, Camels, old Lysanders.
Bombers, fighters, all were there,
Winging 'cross the cold night air.

Propellers spinning silently,
The pilots smiling down at me.
Jet engines, soundless, flying high,
Across the dark and cloudless sky.

Then from my mind, the squadron flew,
Banked to starboard, lost from view.
What message had they brought my way?
What had their presence meant to say?

I didn't know then, don't know now,
But I'll work on it until, somehow,
I find an answer in my head,
To the wraith-like squadron of the dead.

Then should they come again one night,
On silent wings, in silent flight,
Perhaps I'll know just what to say,
To those long-dead souls, of yesterday!

Flightpath of Friendship

Now friends, once enemies of old,
Of those days long ago, let their story be told.
How in darkness of night, they fought battles in the air,
The fighters and bombers, like the hound and the hare!

The knights of the air in their venomous steeds,
All responding in kind to their own nation's needs.
As the bombers droned overhead, lumbering, slow,
So the fighters would scramble, into battle they'd go!

Both sides had secrets, there was Oboe, and Gee,
Würtzburg and Freya helped the fighters to see!
So many were lost in those far away years,
They remember them now, perhaps shed a few tears.

Tears born of memories of friends they once knew,
Brave men, comrades, with whom they once flew.
In aircraft whose names are now part of history,
Junkers and Messerschmitt, Lancaster, Whitley!

Now that war is long ended, those young men have grown old,
But we still can remember those whose story we've told.
The Flightpath of Friendship reaches out 'cross the sea,
Now they're all friends together, and that's how it should be.

Half a century's past since our airmen took flight,
To do battle, now they laugh and tell tales in the night!
With a shake of the hand, and the smile of a friend,
Isn't that how all wars should end?

To commemorate the meeting of the Luftwaffe Night Fighter Pilot's Association, and the RAF Air Gunners Association, Laage, August 2000. The Flightpath of Friendship is an organization dedicated to bringing together the old foes who fought in the skies during World War II, predominantly members of the RAF Air Gunners Association and The Luftwaafe's Night Fighter Pilots Association. These old adversaries now meet regularly as friends, and comrades who, as young men, some with no choice in the matter, once shared the same fears and terrors as they fought the aerial war in the service of their countries.

Hugh's Last Flight

On the night of 21st December 1942 a Wellington of No 3 (Coastal) Operational Training Unit took off from RAF Cranwell on a routine navigation exercise over the North Sea. It was never seen again! The following work is a dramatisation based on letters written by the co-pilot, Flying Officer Hugh Vernon, in the days leading up to the flight. He was just 20 years old. Hugh would not see another Christmas!

This work is dedicated to the memory of Hugh, the crew of W5662, and to all those who served in Coastal Command, Royal Air Force.

Soon be Christmas, letter from home,
Replied straight away, can't waste time.
Flying tonight, nothing special, another bloody exercise!
Mustn't complain though, in a good cause, soon be operational!

Looking forward to leave next month,
Wrote and told them all back home.
Mummy sent wool for Lucy's Christmas, I'll send it off tomorrow.
I'll hide the lipstick in the middle, hope she likes the colour!

Not as cold as yesterday, took a trip to town,
Not to Lincoln, see the bus queues!
Settled for Sleaford, bought some lovely Christmas cards,
I'll write them tomorrow!

'D' for Dogs' the kite for tonight, we flew in her last week,
Another hour we'll be on our way, just got time for tea.
Pre-flight checks, engines warming, God, please keep us safe.
All O.K. now we're rolling, should be back for supper.

Much too dark to see below, North Sea's down there somewhere,
Navigator says "on course", I suppose he must know.
Wait, what's that bang? That flash? Oh no! It can't be, starboard
engine's blown!
Fire spreading, no control, explosion! Hell, we're spinning!

Going down, smoke and flames, spiraling fast, can't move,
Please God don't let it end this way, in a cold and watery grave!
Here it comes, oh Mother I'm scared, it's dark down there, I'm
choking!
They'll never find us way out here, it's dark down
there...............!

In the Aftermath of Battle

It was hot, so very hot, in the aftermath of battle.
The dead lay all around me like so many slaughtered cattle.
Corpses rotting in the sun, blood congealing on the ground,
It was strange, but for a moment I could hear no trace of sound.

A deafening silence, total, absolute, upon the field of death,
Nothing moved, no bird was singing, the wind had lost it's breath!
Was it hours, or just minutes, that I sat there in that place?
Sat beside a fallen friend, who now lay without a face.

I tried to move, my leg hurt, I looked down, I saw the blood,
But I had to get away from there, I had to, if I could.
I crawled past twisted wrecks, not right to call them men anymore,
Their souls were now departed, they had passed through Heaven's door.

It was hot, that's what I remember, the sun was beating down,
In my dread and my confusion I couldn't think, then I lay down.
Couldn't go on any further, I was sickened by the sight,
By the smell of burning flesh, my God, why did we have to fight?

I thought I'd die there in that field, hope was gone, and I was tired,
Was it really a very short time since the first shots had been fired?
Gentle hands came, lifted me softly, were they angels I thought?
Come to claim their harvest of the souls of those who'd fought?

I lay in my delirium for many weeks I'm told,
But of course, I was the lucky one, I survived, I've grown old.
But I remember every face of every man we lost that day,
There were only five of us you see, we were stragglers, lost our way!

It was hot, so very hot, as we crossed that field that day!

Air Gunner

He sought neither glory, nor medals, no fame,
To survive the next flight was the name of the game.
To take off, fly the mission, return in one piece,
Land safely at base, let the tension release!

Through enemy skies, in the darkness of night,
He was part of the aircraft, part of Bomber Command's might!
Besieged by the cold, and assaulted by flak,
Ever watchful for enemy fighter attack!

Ever vulnerable perched in his turret of glass,
Though the view of the skies, at times, was first class!
No time to relax, on constant alert,
If tonight was the night, please God, don't let it hurt!

Nearing the target, attacked by night fighters,
As the guns spat their fire, it was him or those blighters!
No personal hatred, just the will to survive,
To finish the war, to get out alive!

Mission over, home safely, feet on the ground,
Breakfast, then sleep, new dreams to be found.
Maybe dreams of a time not too far ahead,
When the bombing would stop, and we'd all count our dead.

And he thought now and then of the friends who were gone,
Shot from the skies, the unfortunate ones.
Men of courage, like him, though he thought himself less,
Because he'd come home, could still laugh in the mess.

So he carried on flying, continued the tour,
'Til the fighting was over, he was needed no more!
At home once again he relived in his head,
Every flight, every mission, he remembered the dead!

He'd survived, they'd succumbed, and he still bears the scars,
As he honours old comrades, as he looks at the stars.
Now the night sky is peaceful, but his mind sometimes strays,
To those long ago times, to those Bomber Command
days............!

A salute to the Air Gunners of RAF Bomber Command, and to
the memory of those who did not return.

Where Aircraft Once Flew

I look at the places where aircraft once flew,
Where once there were many, now there are but a few.
Many lie empty, disused and untended,
Forgotten it seems, from the day the war ended.

Little Rissington, Swinderby, Syerston, Scampton,
Chivenor, Metheringham, Kenley, and Manston.
Too many to mention them all, but still,
There's just room for Duxford, and old Biggin Hill.

And some of them may have their resident ghosts,
Not there to frighten, hospitable hosts.
For many old airfields have stories to tell,
Of tragedies, heroes, of aircraft that fell!

Of those who returned, and of those who did not,
Of aircraft that just disappeared off the plot.
Of lucky charms lost, and of sweethearts bereaved,
Of crash landings, flame-outs, of airmen retrieved,

From the wreckage of bombers or fighters on fire,
For some 'twas too late, a funeral pyre!
There were crashes at sea, what a place to come down!
For some of those there was no choice, freeze or drown.

There were Poles, there were Czechs, the British, the Aussies,
Flying Spitfires, Hurricanes, Lancasters, Mozzies!
They flew them by night and they flew them by day,
Till the forces of freedom, they finally held sway.

Now the airfields lie empty, and some are all gone,
Redeveloped, ploughed under, some with houses thereon.
So who will remember what happened there?
The men and the women, the knights of the air?

Now with buildings in ruins, and overgrown runways,
They'll host no more air shows, or Battle of Britain days.
It's too bad, but it's true, that no one cares less,
'Bout the places where old airfields lie in distress.

Even though the Second World War ended long ago, many of
the old RAF airfields from those days still survive in one way
or another. Some are still operation RAF bases, others lie in ruins, like Goxhill and Metheringham in Lincolnshire, the concrete
runways cracked and covered with weeds and potholes, in some
cases converted to small industrial estates, or housing develop-
ments, or perhaps with parts of the old bases used as small pri-
vate airfields. Many of these bases are set in the rolling English
countryside, away from towns or villages, and in the midst of
their loneliness it is easy to believe the many stories that exist
of ghostly aircraft and aircrew inhabiting these often desolate
relics, these monuments to the past.

For Those Who Were "There"

Who remembers the "forgotten war"?
Does anyone still care?
'Bout the battle at Imjin River?
Why not ask those who were there?

Ask them of death and dying
As the sound of battle filled the air.
Ask them if they remember,
Ask those men, those who were there!

The Infantry at "Middlesex Hill"
They fought, they did their share.
They won't forget the battle.
They can't, 'cause they were there!

Through the searing heat of Summer,
In Winter, cold beyond compare,
They faced an enemy ever ruthless,
Oh yes, they know that they were there!

There were thoughts of capture, torture,
And other fears they had to bear,
Still they fought the cause of freedom,
At freedoms' calling, they were there!

In the land of morning calm,
Men of land, and sea, and air,
Army, Navy, and the Air Force,
Side by side, all were there!

And in this place so far away,
Was born comradeship so rare,
Where men who fought together
Still remember they were there.

The "forgotten war", Korea,
Now their memories they all share,
If you want to know what happened,
Go on, just ask those who were there!

A salute to the men and women of the British Korean Veterans Association, and to all who fought in freedom's cause during the Korean War 1950-1953.

Who Remembers?

A "little" war, a "dirty" war, but did we not still bleed?
Forgotten now by most, 'cept those whose memories heed
The sound of bullets flying, like swarms of angry bees,
And the driving winter blizzards, bringing strong men to their knees.

Where mortar bombs and napalm desolated nature's plan.
Defend the "Hook", take Pyongyang, the assault on Kowang San.
The spotter planes buzzed overhead, the Auster AOPs,
Unarmed, and unprotected from the guns of the Chinese.

Those swarming hordes of Eastern hell with terrifying screams.
Attacked and fell, attacked again, like demons from your dreams!
Brave men torn asunder, shattered limbs, blood soaked ground.
Migs screaming 'cross the sky above, no-one forgets that sound.

Soldiers of the Commonwealth fought together, side by side.
Through the rain, the mud, the stench of death, men of many nations died.
In the name of liberty they fought, then the World chose to forget.
Because there was no victory, Korea stands divided yet!

But on a bleak hillside somewhere in that far off foreign land
Is a lonely place, where peace now reigns, where the painted crosses stand.
No heroes welcome home for those who heard the final call,
Though they still live on in a memory, someone, somewhere, remembers them all!

Where Poppies Grow

(For my Grandfather and his comrades)

The fields are lush and green now, and silence reigns supreme
And lazy cows graze languidly in this peaceful pastoral scene.
The summer sun shines warmly upon the verdant ground,
Even the gentle summer breeze hesitates to make a sound.

Yet here is where the poppies grow, amongst the grass so green,
Poppies red as the river of blood with which these fields did
teem.
And lying deep beneath the earth sleep those men without a
grave,
A poppy grows here for each one, for us their lives they gave.

Here was where the guns once roared, where trenches thick
with mud
Belched forth the great battalions who sacrificed their blood.
Across these fields they ran and fell in the hell of no-mans land,
And the bodies of the dead sank deep in the mud where none
could stand.

Here were enemies and allies, lost youth lying side by side
Upon the field of battle, where a generation died.
And all the hopes and dreams they carried were suddenly no
more,
And nations mourned, and widows wept at the futility of war.

For when the battles ended, when all was said and done,
Could anyone imagine that anyone had really won?
As mothers cried, and children asked "When's Daddy coming home?"
The poppies grew in red profusion, where the seeds of blood were sown.

Poppies, poppies, everywhere, growing wild and free,
Blowing in the gentle breeze, where so many died for me.
And in the nearby cemetery amongst the myriad crosses,
More poppies grow beside them in remembrance of wars' losses.

Here is where their futures died in the mud, and in the stench,
Last letters written poignantly left in a stinking trench.
Gas and bullets, bayonet steel, death at a strangers' hand,
Tomorrow gone forever here in a foreign land.

The cows still graze in sunshine, in this green and pleasant field,
Where poppies are the finest crop that ever the land can yield.
Every year they blossom in remembrance of the dead,
And with the coming of the evening, each poppy bends its head!

Almost Home

Winging o'er the snow-capped waves,
White horses on the sea.
Winging home to England,
Flying, high and free.

White cliffs 'neath the wingtips,
Green fields far below.
Home beckons by the second,
The only place to go.

A sudden thud, a lurch to port,
Instant pain, confusion reigns.
Losing height, no control,
Blood pumping through the veins.

The fields of home much closer,
Coming up to meet the sky,
No escape, sun shining bright,
A lovely day to die!

Bomb Disposal in The Masons Arms

It must have exploded suddenly
I don't remember much.
Just a flash, and the rush of a mighty wind,
Like an awesome giant's push.

I suppose I was lucky,
I've lived to tell the tale,
Of the bomb in the cellar of the Masons Arms,
Surrounded by kegs of ale.

The building was quite empty,
They'd got everybody out,
Then they heard the ticking,
That's when we got the shout.

The street seemed naught but rubble,
A desolate, awful sight,
Ruined by the rain of death
That had fallen in the night.

That's when we do our bit you see,
In the bloody aftermath.
We arrive, and all the others leave,
Then we face the ticking wrath.

So anyway, there I was,
Just doing what I do,
Until the moment Hell broke loose,
And the UXB just blew!

So many maimed and blown to bits,
But I survived, I'm lucky, me,
The bones and burns will heal they say,
But I just wish that I could see!

Personnel of the Bomb Disposal services daily faced the risks of
death, or serious injury.
To them, this work is dedicated.

Of Men and Cats – June 1940

(Just another 'day at the office' during the Battle of Britain)

He sat there in the morning sun, his trusty pipe in hand,
Lazily, he raised an eye, and watched an aircraft land.
The squadron cat lay sleeping on the crew room window sill,
No need to rush, but later, she'd maybe find a mouse to kill!

The birds were singing cheerily to greet a summer's day,
A fly buzzed round his ear, his hand shooed it away.
While a young man read the news, another scratched his nose,
Two more were playing chess, while another tried to doze.

The day was getting warmer, and then, without preamble,
The telephone rang, and he knew of course, this was the call to scramble!
He ran to where his aircraft waited, in that lovely morning sun,
As he settled in the cockpit, his pulse began to run.

This was it, another sortie, the tenth he'd flown this week,
There'd be more he knew, if he survived the aerial hide and seek.
He followed the directions from controllers on the ground
'Til a thousand feet below him, the enemy bombers were found

He dived and he fired, one went down in flames,
The adrenaline pumped from these aerial games!
Another fired back, his engine was hit,
For a moment he thought that at last, this was it.

He pulled the release, the canopy flew,
He had to get out, knew just what to do.
As he plummeted down, he let out a prayer,
"Let the 'chute open safely, the ground's hard down there".

A tug, then he floated 'neath his mushroom of silk,
Through a cloud that resembled a great lake of milk.
Safely down, soon returned to the airfield once more,
De-briefed, cup of tea, and then, on with the war!

Back to the deckchair, sat in the sun,
How much longer he thought, 'til we'd got this thing won?
In the warm summer sun, the squadron cat stirred,
The young man stroked her head, as she lazily purred...

Cavalry of the Skies

Dedicated to the men of 105 and 107 Squadrons Royal Air Force, who participated in 'Operation Wreckage', the raid on Bremen, 4th July 1941.

'Twas a summers' day in 'forty one, July the 4th, so long ago,
Just a small group of bombers, they took to the air, the ground not far below.
At 'zero' feet they flew ever onward, over the wave-capped sea,
Onward to their target, close to the ground, to a place in history.

Weather imperfect, for the mission that day, no cloud to mask their arrival,
Now was the moment when adrenalin flowed, a fight for very survival.
'Neath the barrage balloons, under telegraph cables, through the deadly, murderous flack,
Ever onward they flew, with no thought for themselves, pressing home their final attack.

No time to think, fire and noise all around, assaulting body and brain,
No quarter asked, and none was given, ever onwards, through that lethal rain.
This was war, tragic, terrible, but the way of the world, all those years ago,
Without thought of self, minds focused and sure, 'cross the target they flew straight and low.

Like a cavalry charge, the squadrons advanced, taking hit after hit from the ground,
How they felt, we can't know, yet they pressed on regardless, the very earth shook with the sound.
Pulverised by the fire from desperate defenders, through the murderous hail they flew,
In the heat of the battle, four aircraft went down, in flames they fell with their crew.

Yet still they advanced, with courage so rare, this cavalry of the sky,
Scooping telegraph wires round tail-planes and fins, so low did the Blenheims fly.
Through their very own 'Valley of Death' they flew, this 'Light Brigade' of the air,
Pressing home their attack, 'til the time came to go, to take leave of the enemy's lair.

No-one can know of the feelings of the men who took part in that raid,
But today we reflect and give thanks in remembrance for the ultimate sacrifice made
By those who failed to return, for whom the sun would never again rise,
And for all the men who in those dark days of war, were our cavalry of the skies!

Another Day in the Jungle

A cacophonous symphony of insect song, which never seems to stop,
The leeches fastened on my legs, harvesting their gruesome crop.
Screams and screeches of bird and beast assault my every sense,
And somewhere out there the enemy waits, in this jungle dark and dense.

Sweat seems to leak from every pore, no escape from this searing heat,
Stifling, strangling, humid, no relief, and no retreat.
Beneath the canopy of trees, still no relief at night,
No sleep, no rest, on full alert, 'case the enemy comes in sight.

A sentry jumps, it's nothing, just a monkey in a tree,
A parrot squawks its shrill alarm, then takes off, flying free.
And down below in the jungle, living the best we can,
We try to sleep, and to survive, all weary, to a man.

Will they find us in the morning, and if they do, what then?
A firefight, a battle, men killing men.
Then another day of waiting, of jungle hide and seek,
Whichever way you look at it, the future's rather bleak.

And when the war is over, will they come and get us out?
Or will we wander here forever, wondering what it was all about?
We're lost in this awful jungle, no idea which way to go,
We've no idea who we'll meet first, it could be friend or foe.

Jungle fever strikes at will, delirium and worse,
And here we are, stuck in this mess, miles from the nearest nurse.
Hell on earth, this putrid jungle, no place for mortal man,
Let's leave it to the bugs and beasts, and get out if we can!

To those who lived, fought and died in the hot, humid and treacherous jungle war in the Far East during World War II.

Kamikaze Reunion

The sweet scent of orange blossom fills the air,
As evening slips into night.
The old man, tired, weary,
Lays down his head to sleep.
And with the sleep, comes the dream once more,
The same, night following night.
Faces from a distant past, float slowly before his eyes.
And he is transported back in time, to a youth of long ago.
They told him he was special, one of the chosen few,
Servant of the Emperor, and he believed, because he must.
The Divine Wind, they would sweep before them,
The enemies of the nation,
Their own self-executioners, no return, but heroes all.
They were all young men, the finest crop,
The flower of a generation.
And now he remembers the moment,
The dread of the final dive.
The screaming of the engine, the rushing of the wind,
The ship in his sights grew ever larger, filling his whole horizon,
He gained speed, diving ever steeper, all sensation suspended,
no thoughts,
Then, in a blinding flash, his world turned upside down.
He hadn't made the sacrifice, his wing had been shot from the
'plane.
He was thrown from the wreck into the cool blue sea,
Somehow, he'd survived.
And now, in his dream, those faces float before him,
Names remembered, some long forgotten, but the faces will al-
ways remain.

They died for a lost cause, they died in vain,
Brave and loyal to the end.
As they flew into the teeth of the enemy guns,
What last thoughts had they the strength to think?
Or, like him, had their minds closed at the moment of imminent demise?
He dreams the dream each and every night,
Sees the faces, hears his own screams,
Wakes in a sweat of survivors guilt,
Breathes deeply the scented air,
And he knows, that the faces will always be there,
In the silent darkness of the night, in the Land of the Rising Sun,
In his nightly Kamikaze re-union.

A Summer's Day in Kosovo

How bright the sun was shining, how loud the birds sang,
As we passed the minefield.

A lazy dog slept in the shade of a tree,
As the refugees filed past.

A scrawny cat chased a scrawnier mouse,
Through the ruins of someone's home.

Outside the little hospital, two boys playing football,
Inside, the doctor completed his latest amputation.

At the pretty lakeside, young women washing clothes,
In the shadow of a burned out tank.

Two old men sat fishing,
A baby cried for milk.

The noon day sun looked down,
Crops withered in the fields.

Tranquillity reigned, it was summer,
A Kosovan summer's day.

Modern warfare, civil wars, and still the dead lie on the ground,
testament to mankind's continued folly.

That Night in 1944

As I walked across that sodden field, near Lincoln, last November,
I saw the crater in the ground, and it was easy to remember.
With stunning clarity they came, those thoughts, those long gone sights,
Of how it was in '44, after one of those long cold nights.

Returning from another 'op, battered, and on fire,
We thought we'd make it back to base, when we saw old Lincoln's spire.
But our poor old Lanc was wounded, too badly to survive,
Harry tried to lift her nose, but she took a fatal dive.

I remember one almighty crash, then flames, in horror I cried,
As all around me in that chaos, three good men, brave men, died.
Good people of the village, the one we'd crashed nearby,
Pulled us from the burning wreck, and I saw those people cry.

Not just for those they'd rescued, nor just for those who'd perished.
For they saw in us their own loved ones, those whose souls they cherished.
Husbands, fathers, sons, and lovers, all gone to fight the war,
Perhaps they wondered, on seeing us, if they'd see them any more.

We were all young men, we were fireproof, we had to think that way,
It wouldn't do to think perhaps, we'd not see another day.
We flew, we bombed, we rested, and then we'd fly again,
All for Mother England, all those brave young men.

That cold night in November, I remember it so well,
A living, burning, nightmare, a vision of earthly hell.
I never flew again you see, after that awful night,
The burns were bad enough but then, my right eye lost its sight.

Strange, how after all this time, in that field in Lincolnshire,
You can still make out the crater, within sight of Lincoln's spire.
I paid a silent homage to the friends I'd lost that night,
I felt their souls were watching me, looking down from Heaven's height.

For all who flew, and fought and died, I let up a silent prayer,
All my memories, my remembrance, all were focused there.
As I looked upon that crater, after all those passing years,
I remembered Johnny, Mike and Sam, and at last, I shed my tears.

Dedicated in gratitude, to all who served in RAF Bomber Command.

Convoy

Beware the predator, she waits, beneath the mantle of the waves.
Waits to send the unprotected to their final, watery graves!
Black widow of the ocean, wolf, harbinger of death,
Beware the predator, she waits, to take away your breath.

Like sheep, slow moving prey appear, nowhere to run, or scatter,
Unarmed, no defences, to the wolf, that didn't matter!
A bright flash lighting up the night, smoke, fire, freezing water,
Still, the others lumbered on, more sheep for the slaughter.

The waves awash with choking oil, drowning souls, the wolf fed well.
Her deadly fish had struck the heart, for a good ship, 'twas death's knell.
Unseen, the wolf retreated, thinking of the next attack,
Aboard the unarmed merchantmen, they knew that she'd be back!

But now, from the darkness, the avenger came, sleek, grey, churning foam.
This hunter would seek the predator, wherever she may roam.
Bows rising through Atlantic waves, the greyhound of the seas,
She'd find the evil harvester of souls, bring the wolf to its knees.

Contact, depth charges, silence, then the sea boiled with the roar,
Explosion underwater, and the wolf would prowl no more!
For the predator, the prey, for the hunter, just another day,
For all who played the game of death, not too much to say!

75% of those who served in the Kreigsmarine's U-Boat branch failed to survive the war in addition to the thousands of allied seamen in merchant ships and naval escorts, destroyers, corvettes and frigates who lost their lives in the Battle of the Atlantic. The vast majority were conscripts under the age of 21, sent into a war they neither wanted nor understood. Losses on both sides were horrendous. This poem is dedicated to all those mother's sons who failed to return to their homes.

No Headstone on a Sailor's Grave

Third day now, and still no sign of any rescue boat,
Please God, how much longer on this ocean must we float.
Poor Lofty's fell asleep again, I'm afraid he's getting weaker.
Truth be told, I think that our chances are getting bleaker.

She went down so very quickly, it happened all so fast.
Torpedo in the hold I think, judging by the blast.
So cold, wet and hungry, no fresh water to drink.
Must keep baling though, don't want this thing to sink.

Lofty seems delirious, he thinks he's home in bed,
Strange how things like this put all these daft things in your
head.
Maybe my mind will start to go, if we're not found quite soon.
Maybe tonight I'll be looking up, and howling at the moon!

I wish someone would find us, I'd kill for a cup of tea.
But all I can see for miles around is nothing but open sea.
Perhaps they'll never find us, don't even know we're here.
Wasn't much time for a mayday call, will anyone shed a tear?

I'm sleepy now, I must admit, can't go on for very long,
I think I'll soon be listening to the sound of Neptune's song.
If anyone should find these words, say a prayer for Lofty and me.
And please, throw a few rose petals on our grave beneath the
sea.

Dedicated to the men of the Merchant Marine, who unselfishly
laid down their lives for their country during the conflict of nations 1939 - 45.

Return to Flanders Fields

Bloodied dressings, sunken eyes, witness to the passage
of the apocalyptic game of death.
The spectre of Flanders fields mirrored in the haunted faces
that spewed from the train.
War-torn, shell- shocked, pain-wracked symbols,
Of a few yards loss or gain.

Rest, young souls of gallantry, flower of a nations youth,
Rest awhile, and heal your wounds, be well again, and soon.
And when your scars are healing well, we'll make heroes of you
again,
We'll send you back to Flanders fields, 'neath the light of that
spectral moon.

A new barrage, the next advance, another yard to make,
You know it makes sense, your country needs you.
Don't worry if a few don't make it, that's war as you know,
But we'll win though we will, because our hearts are strong and
true.

The generals playing soldiers moving pieces on a board.
Far removed from the field of play they watch, and they wait.
Don't panic boys, they know you're the best,
That's why you're the cannon bait!

Return to Flanders fields, the people are with you all.
But don't tell the grim reality to those who've never been.
Hang on the wire, drown in the mud, take a bullet through the
head,
Fall to the gas, young heroes, or just hope that the wound is
clean!

Danger, UXB

They were men like you, men like me,
Though the kind of war they fought,
Was different, every muscle tense,
Every nerve strained and taut.

They fought the bombs that didn't blow,
The unexploded kind.
Never seeking glory,
These men were not that kind!

On windswept beaches, cratered airfields,
City streets, in rain, sun, or snow,
They'd fight the ticking fuses,
Never knowing when they'd blow.

They diced with death on every call out,
Every job could be their last.
Alert for fiendish booby traps,
Take it easy, not too fast!

The lucky ones came through unscathed,
Others paid a price.
A heavy toll in life and limbs.
Chances rarely coming twice!

Unsung heroes every one,
Each unique in his own way,
Sharing untold dangers
Through every working day.

The debt will never be repaid,
How could it ever be?
How do we start to thank those men,
Who fought the UXB!

Dedicated to the RAF Bomb Disposal Service, and to those of all services who have shared in their perilous task.

Shooting at Each Other!

I'm at the front, but I want to go home,
No more this awful place to roam.
The sarge looks like a demented frog,
As well, he treats me like a dog.

Last night I tried to take a pee,
And a sniper took a shot at me!
I can't think straight with all this noise,
They won't let us alone, me and the boys.

We only want to win the war,
And then go home, and fight no more.
But every time we try to charge,
They push us back, including the sarge!

Then he shouts at us some more,
As if it's our fault that we're at war.
Can't he see that we're doing our best,
Here he comes again, can't he give it a rest?

I suppose we're going to charge again,
And try and shoot the enemy's men.
Then they'll shoot back, we'll shoot some more,
It's all becoming quite a bore.

At home now, they'll be having tea,
I wonder if they'll think of me.
Stuck here in this muddy trench,
Assaulted by this awful stench!

Yes, he we go, the sarge is ready,
It'll be 'Come on boys, now, take it steady'.
I wish that I was home in bed,
But I suppose I'll have to charge instead.

So to all the folks back home, bye bye,
To win the war we're off to try.
Sleep soundly, but think of us each night.
Here at the front, doing nothing but fight!

Stop the War, I want to Get Off!

Please stop the war I want to get off,
I've seen enough of death and pain.
Won't someone, somewhere, stop the war,
So we can all go home again?

We didn't want to come here,
We didn't want to fight.
Why did we come? We'll never know,
But someone thought it right.

It seems so very long ago,
We were young, and looked ahead.
Now we all feel old and weary,
And a lot of us are dead!

So won't someone back home please spare us a thought?
Won't someone hear our plea?
Please stop the war, it's time to go home,
For all the Tommies, and me!

Letter to a Loved One

Don't forget to wave my dear,
when the bombers go over at night,
It might be me in one of them,
you know, my dear, it might.

I can't let you know when we're flying of course,
security you see,
But the fact that you're down there watching the planes,
is quite a comfort to me.

I hope that soon dear, I'll be granted some leave,
maybe a day or two,
And then I'll be home just as fast as I can,
home my darling, to you.

We'll go for a walk in the country perhaps,
then maybe take in a show,
Do all that we can in the short time we have,
'til the time comes for me to go.

Until then I'll keep going, be thinking of you,
every moment I can,
From the day that I met you I've always known dear,
that I'm a lucky man.

Thanks for the scarf that you sent me last month,
I fly with it every night,
The boys pull my leg, call me "Biggles" you know,
they say that I look quite a sight.

But when we're out on a mission,
it helps to feel closer to you,
As well there's the warmth, it gets so cold up there,
I don't know how I don't get the 'flu.

Just four trips to go and we'll finish our tour,
though it still seems a long way to go,
By the way, Stan got married last week, to Elaine,
she's quite a beauty, you know!

It's getting dark dear, and I must away,
there's still a war to be fought,
I'll see you quite soon, then we'll talk more,
as long as our tour's not cut short!

So don't forget to wave my dear,
when the bombers go over at night,
It might be me in one of them,

you know, my dear, it might!

Who's Winning the War?

If I fall, I shall not go home.
I shall lie here forever 'neath this foreign soil.
Not a thought to stir the heart,
Brings no comfort to the soul.

Will I be for all time just a memory,
When the guns have stopped their cacophonous roar,
When the bombs stop falling,
Will I be an ember in the mind of someone, somewhere?

How many lie already,
'Neath this rain soaked sodden acre?
Do the brass up in their chateaux really care?
Do they even know we're here?

Cold, and wet, clinging mud,
Do they think that we can't feel?
Harry drowned in mud last night,
What a way to win a war!

Still, must be patriotic,
Wouldn't do to complain too much.
After all, we're winning aren't we?
Tell me we're winning, please!

Unknown Soldiers

'Twas not so long ago, that I was very much like you.
My body young and vital, filled with life and dreams anew.
Then came obliteration, the bomb blast hurt my head.
Now I look down at what's below, it appears that now I'm dead.

There's not much left of what was me, just pieces, burned and
black,
When the boys go home, I won't be there, there's not enough
left to take back.
My family will shed a tear, my friends may miss me too,
But will I ever be much more than a fleeting memory to you?

Just an unknown man in a uniform, who went to fight the war.
Who once worked hard for his dear old Dad, in his local gro-
cer's store.
But then, to everyone back home, we're almost all unknown.
You only know your own kin, or your friends, with whom
you've grown.

Oh look, there goes another one, another bomb, another life,
Another unknown soldier won't be going home to his wife.
We didn't want to die, we wanted most of all to live,
Not end up looking down, at all the pain that war can give.

Please remember when you think about the men that you have
known,
Remember for a moment, all of us, to you, unknown.
Remember that to someone, we were husbands, lovers, sons,
Until the day the war came, and we marched to face the guns!

The Sweating Man

(A salute to the bomb disposal crews of World War II)

December 1942, the frost clung tight to the land,
A biting cold gripped the earth, draining blood from foot to hand.
But sweat marked the brow of the man in the hole,
As he offered up a prayer for his mortal soul.

He didn't think himself brave, just an ordinary guy,
As he looked up from that hole at the grey morning sky.
He paused for a moment, then took a deep breath,
Then prepared to do battle with this cargo of death!

He surveyed his enemy, silent, and black.
A remnant of the Luftwaffe's night time attack.
Knowing the danger, he began to remove
Soil from the fuses, a delicate move!

Oh so very carefully, he examined what he saw,
Then, with infinite care, the sweating man continued his war.
With his stethoscope he listened, for the ticking of the fuse,
Still sweating despite the cold, carefully picked the right spanner to use.

He paused a moment, drew a breath, his mouth as dry as sand,
He looked down, just to check, for any shaking of his hand.
He had to get it right first time, he knew he had no margin of error.
Deep inside he felt, but didn't show, the slightest tinge of terror.

He'd lived with danger now for as long as he remembered,
He didn't want to end his war blown up, dismembered.
So with steady, careful hands, he went about his task,
The fuse removed, the bomb made safe, his face a sweat lined mask.

No celebrations afterwards, just a quick 'Well done"
Then a cup of tea, relax a while, there'd soon be another one.
As he wiped away the sweat, he suddenly noticed he was cold,
The frost still lay upon the ground, and the sweating man felt old.

Postcard from Stalingrad

Love me only as a fleeting sunbeam, transitory, brief,
For my life may be extinguished leaving you with tragic grief.
Love me only as a sunlit day, as ripples in the sand,
As one whose essence flits across the ever changing land.

Though the war that brought us close together now keeps us apart,
My darling keep my memory safe deep within your heart.
Until the day when soon I hope I'm in your arms again.
Back home and safe forever, keep me in your thoughts 'til then.

So love me as a Summer's day, so warm and full of life,
And then one day I'll come home again, and take you for my wife.
But just in case the Winter comes, and I'm left here in the cold,
Remember how you loved me, I who never did grow old!

Recruiting at the Theatre

All you brave boys out there, step forward for the war.
They need you at the front me lads, all of you and many more.
Join up me bonny heroes, we're all behind you in what you do,
March to glory all you Englishmen, your King and your country
need you..

We'll watch you marching as you go, as the colours you proudly
raise,
And we'll keep the home fires burning, as your efforts we all
praise.
You'll fight for freedom for our land, for God is on our side,
You'll have a grand time over there, as you turn the enemy tide.

The army will look after you, for you're the best in all the land,
And you'll soon be home once more me lads, back in dear Eng-
land.
Don't hang back, see the sergeant, he'll sign you at a stroke,
Don't be put off by his stern expression, he's a really decent
bloke.

And when the guns are firing, and the sound of battle rages,
Remember that we're proud of you, you'll be heroes in history's
pages.
So all you brave boys out there, step forward for the war,
They need you at the front me lads, all of you and many more.

A Wartime Stroll

Come, walk with me in the shadows of war,
Walk through the memories of those gone before.
Through days of adversity, nights filled with fear,
When so many were lost, all of whom we held dear.

Through the remnants of men's' bodies, twisted and shattered,
When winning the next battle seemed all that mattered.
Let's walk through the minefield of mangled emotion,
Bred by gunfire, and bombing, wars' grievous commotion!

Should we tell all our young folk? Yes let them be told,
How their forefathers fought, how some never grew old!
Let them learn of the sounds and the carnage of battle,
Of total destruction, the sound of deaths' rattle.

Walk through rivers of blood, through the torrent of pain,
Through a bomb ravaged city, a war-damaged brain!
Let us stroll through the cemeteries, littered with crosses,
Remember the fallen, the "acceptable losses".

Young men left for the fight, they were all brave and bold,
The lucky ones came back, but by then, they'd grown old.
They'd seen far too much, more than mere man should see,
Lost youth and innocence, cut down as a tree.

And let's take a walk 'cross an old battlefield,
Where no quarter was given, where no-one would yield.
Where men died, in agony, shot where they stood,
Where the earth turned to red, as it stained with their blood!

Remember the men and the women who died,
As we walk through the river of tears that were cried.
'Neath the earth, and the sea, lie so many unfound,
Without grave or memorial in Gods' hallowed ground

Let's walk back now, the present's a much better place,
But just close your eyes, see an old soldiers' face.
Don't forget them, the men who went off to the war,
For the future we live in, their own they forswore!

A Nightmare Journey

(Warsaw Ghetto)

In his dreams, he's just a boy again,
Ten years old,
And terrified.

Sees the men with guns,
Hears the shots, the screams,
He's terrified.

Rats scurrying across the street,
Hunger gnawing at his insides,
And he's terrified.

The dead horse by the roadside,
Scavengers strip it bare, fighting for the entrails,
He's so terrified.

The sound of those lorries in the night
More screams, shots, beatings,
So terrified.

A railway wagon, no food, no water,
The stench of human garbage,
He was never so terrified.

No idea where he's going,
Ten years old, confused,
And totally terrified.

A snowscape of evil, strange smoke in the sky,
Dogs barking, men in black shouting,
Unbelievably terrified.

His mind can't take any more,
The man wakes, shaking, sweating,
And terrified.

Remembrance

Remember the fallen, the honoured dead,
In silent prayer, with lowered head.
They gave of their all, they gave up their lives,
And remember as well all the war-widowed wives.

Fathers of children, all some mothers sons,
Taken from life by the bombs, and the guns.
No joyous salute, nor heroes return,
Just an empty chair somewhere, a story to learn.

Of young men who proudly went off to the wars,
Leaving families, friends, leaving England's shores.
Many dying with glory, though seeking no fame,
Now lying at rest, in a grave with no name.

Given peace from the tumult, in the Lord's gentle care,
Lie the soldiers, the sailors, those who fought in the air.
Those who sacrificed all for the things they held dear,
Let us honour the memory, of those no longer here.

To all those of many nations who served on land, on and under
the sea, and in the air, and to those who waited for them to
return, "We will remember them."

Contents

Lightning Source UK Ltd.
Milton Keynes UK
UKHW052206230221
379219UK00021B/1337/J